THE PENGUIN POETS

LIKE WINGS

Born and raised in Rochester, New York,
Philip Schultz has taught at several univer-
sities and is now on the faculty of New York
University. His poetry has appeared in *The
New Yorker*, *American Review*, *The Na-
tion*, and *Partisan Review*, and his short
stories in the *Iowa Review*, the *Transatlan-
tic Review*, and other periodicals. He has
recorded his poems for the Lamont Library
at Harvard University and for Spoken Arts,
Inc. In 1976 he won *The Nation*–Y.M.H.A.
Discovery Award as well as a grant from the
New York State Creative Artists Public
Service Program. Of his work, Grace
Schulman, poetry editor of *The Nation* and
director of the Poetry Center, 92nd Street
Y.M.H.A., has said: "Philip Schultz's po-
etry is remarkable for its passion and con-
trol, its precision and care. He is a master at
transmuting the rhythms of contemporary
speech, and at combining them with his own
haunting original music. I feel that he is at
the beginning of an important career."

LIKE WINGS

Poems by Philip Schultz

PENGUIN BOOKS

WITHDRAWN

CARL A. RUDISILL LIBRARY
LENOIR-RHYNE UNIVERSITY

PS
3569
.C5533
L5
1978

Penguin Books Ltd, Harmondsworth, Middlesex, England
Penguin Books, 625 Madison Avenue, New York, New York 10022, U.S.A.
Penguin Books Australia Ltd, Ringwood, Victoria, Australia
Penguin Books Canada Limited, 2801 John Street, Markham, Ontario, Canada L3R 1B4
Penguin Books (N.Z.) Ltd, 182–190 Wairau Road, Auckland 10, New Zealand

March 2012

First published in the United States of America and Canada in simultaneous hardcover and
paperback editions by The Viking Press and Penguin Books 1978

Copyright © Philip Schultz, 1972, 1973, 1975, 1976, 1977, 1978
All rights reserved

LIBRARY OF CONGRESS CATALOGING IN PUBLICATION DATA
Schultz, Philip.
   Like wings.
   I. Title.
PS3569.C5533L5   811'.5'4   78-18443
ISBN 0 14 042.264 1

Printed in the United States of America by The Book Press, Brattleboro, Vermont
Set in CRT Bodoni Book

With special gratitude to the Corporation of Yaddo and the MacDowell Colony, where
many of these poems were written, and to the New York Council on the Arts (Creative
Artists Public Service Program) for a grant to work on this book

ACKNOWLEDGMENTS
The American Review: "Strangers in Old Photographs" and "The Artist and His Mother:
After Arshile Gorky." *Barataria:* "Knots" and "I Don't Think." *Blacksmith Anthology:*
"For the Moose." *Centering: A Magazine of Poetry:* "Photographs on the Mountain,"
"Night Waters," and "Song." *Choice:* "Somewhere in Spain." *The Falcon:* "A
Modigliani Nude." *The Nation:* "Salt Flats," "Gogol's Coat," "There Is," "Garage Sale,
Last Day in May," "Cézanne," and "Laughter." *New York Quarterly:* "What I Don't
Want." *The New Yorker:* "Waking in the Cold," "Onionskin for the New Year," "A
Prayer," "Like Wings," "For the Wandering Jews," and "The Gift." *Partisan Review:*
"Main Streets" (Parts I–V). *Pequod:* "Main Streets" (complete poem). *Poetry:* "Savage
Feelings," "Darwin, Tortoises, Galapagos Archipelago & New Hampshire," and "For My
Father."

Except in the United States of America,
this book is sold subject to the condition
that it shall not, by way of trade or otherwise,
be lent, re-sold, hired out, or otherwise circulated
without the publisher's prior consent in any form of
binding or cover other than that in which it is
published and without a similar condition
including this condition being imposed
on the subsequent purchaser

WITHDRAWN

CARL A. RUDISILL LIBRARY
LENOIR-RHYNE UNIVERSITY

For my mother & in memory of my father

CONTENTS

FOR THE WANDERING JEWS

MAIN STREETS   45

THE GIFT

FOR THE WANDERING JEWS

FOR THE WANDERING JEWS

This room is reserved for wandering Jews.
Around me, in other rooms, suitcases whine
like animals shut up for the night.

My guardian angel, Stein, fears sleeping twice
in the same bed. Constancy brings Cossacks in the dark, he thinks.
You don't explain fear to fear. Despair has no ears, but teeth.

In the next room I hear a woman's laughter
& press my hand to the wall. Car lights burn
my flesh to a glass transparency.

My father was born in Novo-Nikolayevka, Ekaterinoslav Guberniya.
Like him, I wear my forehead high, have quick eyes, a belly laugh.
Miles unfold in the palm of my hand.

Across some thousand back yards his stone
roots him to the earth like a stake. Alone in bed,
I feel his blood wander through my veins.

As a boy I would spend whole nights at the fair
running up the fun house's spinning barrel toward its magical top,
where I believed I would be beyond harm, at last.

How I would break my body to be free of it,
night after night, all summer long, this boy climbing
the sky's turning side, against all odds,

as though to be one with time,
going always somewhere where no one had been before,
my arms banging at my sides like wings.

THE ARTIST & HIS MOTHER:
AFTER ARSHILE GORKY

Such statuesque immobility; here we have it:
the world of form. Colors muted, a quality
of masks with fine high brows. Light & its absence.
Alchemy. The hands are unfinished. But what
could they hold? The transitory bliss
of enduring wonder? Mother, Mother & Son;
here we have it: consanguinity. The darkness
inside color. Space. In the beginning there was space.
It held nothing. What could it hold? Time?
The continuum? Mother & Son, forms suspended
in color. Silence. Her apron a cloud
of stillness swallowing her whole. Her eyes
roots of a darker dimension. Absence. Here we have it:
the world of absence. Light holds them in place.
The pulse of time is felt under the flesh,
the flesh of color. Continuum. You feel
such immensity. The anger of form. The woman
locked in the Mother; the man in the Son; the Son
in the Mother. Their hands do not touch. What
could they touch? Here we have it: the world
of gift. The gift too terrible to return. But
how could it be returned? In the beginning
there was anger. Mother & Son. The islands of time.
The passion to continue. Such statuesque immobility.
The hands, the hands cannot be finished.

THE STRANGER IN OLD PHOTOS

You see him over my Uncle Al's left shoulder
eating corn at a Sunday picnic & that's him
behind my parents on a boardwalk in Atlantic City

smiling out of focus like a rejected suitor
& he's the milkman slouched frozen crossing our old street
ten years before color & his is the face above mine in Times Square

blurring into the crowd like a movie extra's
& a darkness in his eyes as if he knew his face would outlast him
& he's tired of living on the periphery of our occasions.

These strangers at bus stops, sleepwalkers
caught forever turning a corner—I always wondered who they were
between photos when they weren't posing & if they mattered.

It's three this morning, a traffic light blinks yellow yellow
& in my window my face slips into the emptiness between glares.
We are strangers in our own photos. Our strangeness has no source.

OF THE PIT

For Norman

Listen, it hasn't been all wild dancing, Brother.
Lifting tables in my teeth & kicking dishes off the wall.
I haven't spent all my time chasing widows with porpoise eyes
or watching geese scorch the dawnlit horizon. Sure,
I'm part Cossack by nature if not inclination,
but I have more serious ambitions. Let me tell you, Peachpit,
I was also frightened of horsemen as a boy, I knew
the hollow of my sisters' skirts, the deepest grass,
the striped dark of trapdoors, you bet your last kulak.
I was acquainted with the raw unsalted bite of fear
& would swing head over balls from branches too thin to whittle.
I peeped through back windows & gave lip service to shadows
& dressed down not to incite the roaming goyim, Comrade.
Only by moonlight was my true nature revealed
& then only by profile. Maybe I was callow, but with flair!
Sure my papa used to board up the windows
& never loved the next town, but I'm no dark-age myopic!
I do ninety pushups lefthanded & ask the ladies
if I'm a bentback hoarder, hah! I've fought the wars
& sired whole tribes of draft dodgers, so pass the vodka, Boychick.
You see that cloud of dust lifting off the plains?
That's me coming all the way from Egypt
with the incense of darkest knowledge in my nose,
the raw ambition & oil of know-how between my legs.
That's me wearing the teeth of pagans, stones from the Black Sea,
round my neck. For I am of the pit, the blossoming wart
on the nose of wildest desire.
I eat whole hogs raw & without the salt of guilt.
I killed Christ, I admit it!

THE BAR MITZVAH

King for the night! the rabbi cried.
My pockets heavy with savings bonds, I stole kisses
from every woman old enough to recognize what was starting.
Oh we bunny-hopped round mountains of chopped liver
& sliced cakes big as Buffalo. Uncle Hy explained success:
Mexican Hat Dance with the best! Uncle Lou showed
his war wounds & Aunt Becky pulled me close: "A word
to the near-wise. Responsibility's the road to happiness.
Life's not all corn on the cob, darlink!" Later, I pulled
Susan into a back room. But she turned away. "We'd only
hate ourselves in the morning," she sighed. So I went
up to the roof & tightroped the ledge & threw up
my first whisky eight floors down onto Uncle Herb's new Buick.
Downstairs my father counted our loot in the empty hall
while my mother stared at her emerald gown as I whirled
an eighty-four-year-old girl between tables, her braids bouncing!
Round & round we went, the room swaying without stop.
Suddenly it was Russia in her eyes & everything about to begin.
Myself a man for the rest of my life!

FOR MY BIRTHDAY

Home first night in years, I stand tall before the door
remembering the photo dated 1945 in windshield snow,
my father's pudgy-cheeked smile heralding my first hour.
Passing through, I waltz my mother round the kitchen

& wash her face with snow all the way from New Mexico.
Alone with his wife, I feel his presence slurp coffee
still too hot, his keys banging forgotten on his hurrying hip.
Father, I've come back to fix her storm windows

& hang the can opener within reach. I'm twenty-six today
& something has slowed in me, is more careful now.
I won't slam the door & run off to Tangier, I don't think.

My one key bangs on my hip as we turn between stove & table
five inches off the floor. Yes, I was the light going out
of you the winter night of '45, but for better or worse,
I just dropped by to say hello & waltz her once for old times.

SONG FOR A SHEARED-BEAVER COAT

Two-fisted old woman, packed chin to boots
in the ratted shimmer of inherited fur,
four feet ten, she ran a house of men
with her Yiddish-Russian-American tongue
& a will that argued with the dead,
America was five tailors & a sway-back mare
when she arrived & it stayed the size
of her neighborhood, this old mother
whose stone knees rocked me until I howled,
who scalded ants she feared would eat her house
& pounded meat bloodless Fridays, rocking the floors,
who pinned me to the wall with her Baltic blue eye
& wore a fur coat all summer—I still
feel her heart that July afternoon
as I carried her down a silence that wouldn't break
& set her into the fold of her bones in an iron bed,
with her wild stare & steel grip, Grandma,
I understood for the first time that life
wasn't four blocks long between God
& the Monday bread.

LETTER FROM JAKE: AUGUST 1964

Never mind that uncle business my name is Jake.
In college they try every thing there is this girl
at Wegmans supermarket who is to busy to join
protests who is right takes more than me
to figure out. Cohen died last Monday. He owned
the deli on Joseph Ave. The democrat running
for supervisor is a Puerto Rican. Don't ask me why.

You are young and have to take things
as they come. Some day you will find your
real niche. I wrote poetry to but this July
I'm a stagehand 40 years. I've seen every movie
Paramount made believe me. Now theres a union
but I remember when you was happy just to work.
Meantime have a ball. Yrs truly now has kidney
trouble plus diabetic condition, heart murmur,
cataract in rt eye. Yr mother Lillian is well to.
Cohen was just 58. We went to school together. Loews
is closing in October. If you ask me the last
five rows was no good for cinemascope.

                                    Yrs truly,
                                        Jake

THE SECRET

The August heat of beef & red drains at my feet
as I lug ninety pounds from freezer to the mouths of trucks
& rip stony flesh with the hook of my fist & fear being hooked
& sliced & hung on steel ribs & noon the trucks hiss like beasts
& the men hold lunchbags swollen like brains & their breath is white
& at night my mother embraces my father's outline in her bed
& she combs her hair & her hair is death & she paints her lips
& her lips are death & I walk all night & there is a secret
in the silence of the stars & at dawn I step into the bus
with men who stare at their hands & it is in their eyes black
with sleep & in the arms hanging by strings & a girl steps up
& it is in her eyes & I want to tell her the trucks & the blood
& the moaning that lasts all night & we sway hooked by straps
& our hips touch & she smiles as if being kissed from her feet up.

WHAT I DON'T WANT

Die slouched & undecided in a girlie show
watching the lambs eat the wolves.
Sit talking Kafka this Kafka that
(that bugfaced sword-swallower!).
Play deaf & dumb in Chicago.
Chew the fat of the land while looking
up somebody's leg for the right word, ever again.
Cross the Golden Gate Bridge on a bus
listening to the guy ahead say: Doesn't it look
like a G-string all lit up, Fran!
Die in the house where I was born,
a happy man.

I want, Lord, to die with Neruda & Chaplin
naked & sinful
eating cheese so old it sings on my tongue.

THE GIRLIE SHOW

The house lights shimmer
into an insect haze. Mama Fats

opens the petals of her thighs
& stuns

every woman's son
with her shaved eye of God.

My shadow
left burning to its knees.

SAVAGE FEELINGS

I sweat & toss all night.
I stare at walls as if I cared for them.
I constantly ask myself why L drinks so little
& why K is always off sailing.
I get urges (for my old room above the junkyard)
which I can't control at the best of times.
My friends are knocking themselves off so fast
I call hourly before meeting anyone for lunch.
Everything has become a matter of time.
Posters on buses say: Keep It Up!
I cannot keep it up.
Nobody I know can keep it up.
Late at night there is this fear
of suddenly nothing which comes out of nowhere.
Everything is turning out just as I suspected.

PLAYING DEAD

I lie on my stomach in hot sand.
I bury my face, hands & legs.
They come out of the waves & crawl
through the sand with knives. They find me.
They turn me over & listen for breath.
They open my eyes & mouth.
They dare me to come out.
But I am a toad meshed in ferns.
A fist without bones.
I am the last child.
The prince of death.
Naked in the stony light.

A PRAYER

Downstairs, a woman
is singing. Like a leaf,

I press my ear to the floor.
It is a splendid thing!

But I am too drunk
with the hours of myself,

too much in love
with the knuckles of my right hand,

to climb inside her song.
Bless her hundred daughters,

whose praise she sings. Bless
this floor turning

to water. Child of angels,
bless your tongue,

which is promise.

WAKING IN THE COLD

For Howard

My brain loves itself too much, I think.
It dreams it can fly. My body prefers
the cold, its knives.

Inside my body, my body ties knots
in the blood's light, rubs cells to fire.
It loves to come downstairs where
Marie smells of coffee & has the fires going.
It loves the chortling.

For myself I prefer not to ask my feet
why one goes before its brother.
I prefer to stand at this notched window
with the fire at my back, watching new snow
grow across sloping fields toward spring.

SALT FLATS

The sky ends where the salt begins.
Light notches the eye
& the whiteness listens
like a mirror
you turn your back to
in the dark.

I DON'T THINK

it's choice or love of punishment. How can it be?
These men & women aren't in love with their wretchedness.
It isn't fear of death. This I know for a fact.
I have seen an old man fall into his face & lie whispering
to his blood & not care. Something inside just stopped.
Curling under trucks or huddling round burning trash
away from January rain isn't choice. It can't be.
I have waited in line frightened the window would shut
before I got bus fare & food stamps. But I was a tourist,
playing poor. Not having money is not poor the way
they are poor. I have seen a wedge-faced man hold his fist
in fire, then lift it smoking to the light & laugh
as if nothing could hurt him any more. No, it can't be choice.
Something stops & won't get up & no longer cares.
Hope is just another word. Like spite.

ONIONSKIN: FOR THE NEW YEAR

Already there is as much behind as ahead.
Knowing this we link arms, here, high
on the cusp of the city, in the vicinity
of this moment. Refugees, we strain
for a glimpse of the New World, ready
to astonish any absolute. Below,
the Charles spins its sinuous flow
of detail under bridges of pure reason
as we smile for the gap-toothed honey
who snaps us for posterity. Yes,
it has become impossible to be human;
we agree that we are what is good
about time & sing for all we're worth,
our whisky gargle the unraveling onionskin
of too many near collisions.

SOMEWHERE IN SPAIN

I lift out of the dream of being nowhere in particular
& stare into the dark. The girl beside me is dark
from the sun & lies curled on her stomach like a child.
I rise & go to the window & look up at the red moon
& white houses spread like bones over the black hills.
Once in a museum I couldn't breathe for fear
of being without time or place & I stood wrapped
in my arms repeating the months of the year, everywhere
a system of halls. Now two women in black shawls pass
down the ancient brick & I recall that I am somewhere in Spain,
high in the hills near the sea & laugh as the girl calls me
from her sleep in German by someone else's name.

KNOTS

I cannot tie my tie right.
I stand at the window cursing my hands.
Once I could not tie my shoes.
I wanted my mother to.
I wanted her down on her knees for love of me.
I wanted the smell of her hair in my face.

Marie enjoys watching me knot my tie.
She knows it is something I must do alone.
Even after such amazing contact.
At her touch the nerves in my fingertips jump
like fish
flipping upstream against all common sense.

GARAGE SALE, LAST DAY IN MAY

This old farmer rubs a burnt-orange tongue
over oak my father's father smuggled in from Russia.
His eyes glow. We shake hands.
The table is his for twenty dollars.

His thick-legged daughter flirts
with a rusted powder tin your mother hammered
out of sardine cans. Your wife's? she wants to know.
It's hers. She curtsies at the door.

The lady from Paw Paw bought your black lace shawl.
I think she thinks it'll turn her eyes green again.
She held it to her cheek & laughed.
She would've waltzed me up Main Street if I'd let her.

Beginning takes time & we're always beginning.
I walk the block measuring each step
as if it were my last. Above,
stars roll past like couples, silent with sexual grace.

GOGOL'S COAT

I mean to imagine the wilderness
where trees are not trees when touched.
The lover's longing when he wakes
with his head on her belly, his hand lost
in that dark. How then most of all
the trees are not trees when touched.

I think of Gogol's clerk whose desire
for a skin so exquisite all Russia's winds
would brush off his chest like a kiss
is the lover's to be inside
where the trees are trees when touched.

How as he stands before the mirror
& sees himself inside the coat, at last,
the salt of stars on his tongue, he remains
himself the clerk when touched, but loves
the coat which cannot be forgiven.

WOULD YOU BELIEVE

that after all this time & place I saw your face
in the face of the woman sleeping beside me this morning
& your name caught in my throat like a knot of breath,

that once there was nothing I wouldn't have done,
no place I wouldn't have gone for you,
that you were the reason why clocks of all kinds worked,

that I can still see the identical beauty marks on each cheek,
the way your knees knocked when you ran,
the bright green-eyed smile that left alarm salesmen speechless,

that we give so much of ourselves that first time
our otherness burns like an incision on the small of our backs
& does not stop,

that you are the blood that swirls in me like a Nijinsky,
that wild acrobat of fever, who must always live an inch higher
in the impossible air of my loving?

PHOTOGRAPH ON THE MOUNTAIN

Six people wrapped
in one another
like strange flowers.
Rapt, open-eyed, we
are pulling closer
even as we pull apart.
A midsummer day
with sky the blue-
green of fields. You
feel a kind of fire
lifting out of rock.
Out of rock, I say.

THE ELEVATOR

This elevator lugged Teddy Roosevelt
when they both were new. Now I count stars
in the skylight as it jerks into the sudden light
down hallways & hug groceries like a thief his loot
when it stops in the dark between floors. Often
it howls climbing, sings falling. Someone
on the fifth floor loves chicken fat & Brahms;
the worst soprano in Cambridge lives on the third.
The man above me taps goodnight on his floor but
doesn't know me in the street. The girl down the hall
drops her head if I smile in the elevator; she knows
I watch her run to work each morning from my window.
After dinner I stand there with my hands folded behind
as I imagine Mr. Roosevelt stood, watching the lights
come on along the spine that is Massachusetts Avenue at night.

WANT

There is always a beautiful moment.
Often a woman owns it. Bats her green eyes. Time
vanishes. You stand in the back row, complain

about such ache deep in the belly. So
what is he looking for now, roaming
the woods just before dawn? Doesn't

he know that the perfection of time
isn't found in a woman's thigh—
that the ideal tastes of blood? Soon

the field will burst with invention,
the dew will fire. Don't want too badly
or you just might get it, fathers tell us.

But this field is too wide to encompass
with arms & grass waves in tremors
vulnerable as flesh. My shirt soaked

to the spirit, my breath spheres
of light & dark—Papa, I'm in love again.
I pitch with the last echoing star.

THE CROCODILE

The crocodile floats on its tail & rolls its yellow eyes.
It licks my hand like a tease.
It is the sorriest creature & knows it.
Suddenly its jaws close around my arm & we roll down a street of trees.
Our passion gives off a black smoke.
I feel an enormous strength & squeeze its head until its jaws open.
Its tiny arms lift imploringly.
It is early May.
There is only one of us.
I experience the exhilaration of choice.
I go down the street in search of a bride.

A MODIGLIANI NUDE

I didn't see her come in; she
sat on my desk & smiled,
just like that.

Pink flesh, long chestnut hair
lit the sepia walls. Christ, I said,
it's a real Modigliani nude!

So I pinched her dimpled knee
& took her out to the park
& mounted her under the shade of the world's biggest morning-glory

just as the mayor walked by
with his blue invalid wife
who smiled about the nicest smile I'd ever seen.

Monsieur, she whispered, this
is not bad, but please once again for luck!
Later we went down to the sea

where the gulls called, Good for you!
She gave me the kiss of my life
& ran into the bluest water waving good-by.

Now I sit typing this poem
with my eye on the door, just in case.
The strangest fire up my spine.

NIGHT WATERS

We swim the moonless Gulf Stream.
The water is warm & salty.
The stars guide us.
We move in & out of ourselves like lovers.
We go over the edge
we always know is there.

FOR THE MOOSE

Tania must place her hands on my skull,
one above the other, to better hear the truth.
We are discussing the art of poetry. Eight
years old, she chews her lip & squints. Who's
my moose? she wants to know. Does she just
hand one over or what? Last night she dreamed
her bed was full of frogs, then her ship sank.
Do poems give nightmares? Funny, I say, but
I had the same dream. This breaks her up.
Well how about God; do you always have to put
Him in? No more than three-legged horses, I say.
They get equal time. Which brings the big one:
Will she be rich & famous before she's fifteen?
Will they hang her picture in the A&P?
Will she have to fall in love every day &
come down with some fatal disease? Her father
said poets led sad lives. I put my arms around
her & think: Stick to new math & somersaults
& if you must write, write historical novels
about gorgeous queens who give up whole kingdoms
for love. But say: Tania, your hair's on fire,
your eyes are poached eggs! So she punches me,
which means that's it for today. I watch her
go down the cinderblock with her hands high
on her head as if feeling a poem bake.
Darling, may the good moose be kind.

SONG

Down twilight roads
two boys walk happy
as friends come &
they are four waving
at old women black
in doorways girls
smiling in windows
the rhythm is great
the walking talking
as friends come &
they are seven &
happy to be so many
it is the way to be
here in the summer
streets of Guadalajara.

FLEAWORTS

Today my hand
won't come out
of my sleeve;
my feelings
wrong for my clothes.
Today a fleawort
has blossomed
in my hair
& a man
I don't know
passes me in a crowd,
whispers
good luck.

SAN FRANCISCO REMEMBERED

In summer the polleny light bounces off the white buildings
& you can see their spines & nerves & where the joints knot.
You've never seen such polleny light. The whole city shining
& the women wearing dresses so thin you see their wing-tipped hips
& their tall silvery legs alone can knock your eye out.
But this isn't about women. It's about the city of blue waters
& fog so thick it wraps round your legs & leaves glistening trails
along the dark winding streets. Once I followed such a trail
& wound up beside this redheaded woman who looked up & smiled
& let me tell you you don't see smiles like that in Jersey City.
She was wearing a black raincoat with two hundred pockets
& I wanted to put my hands in each one. But forget about her.
I was talking about the fog which steps up & taps your shoulder
like a panhandler who wants bus fare to a joint called The Paradise
& where else could this happen? On Sundays Golden Gate Park
is filled with young girls strolling the transplanted palms
& imported rhododendron beds. You should see the sunset
in their eyes & the sway, the proud sway of their young shoulders.
Believe me, it takes a day or two to recover. Or the trolleys clanking
down the steep hills—why you see legs flashing like mirrors!
Please, Lord, please let me talk about San Francisco. How
that gorilla of a bridge twists in the ocean wind & the earth
turns under your feet & at any moment the whole works can crack
& slip back into the sea like a giant being kicked off his raft
& now, if it's all right, I would like to talk about women . . .

THERE IS

There is the house I build that is never finished.
The rooms which are never large enough.

There is the weather outside this house.
The light which is never bright enough.

All my life I am all my life going from this house
into this weather & the dark between.

THE APARTMENT-HUNTER

The longing that moves me is a second, heavier body.
In dark rooms I stare at buildings which mirror other buildings.

The single hanger swaying in closets is always the same hanger.
I press my ear to walls & hear my own echo.

Each empty apartment is a legacy of silence.
I meet myself on stairs & pass without nodding.

THE DEAD REMEMBER

the black moons of their fingernails
their cheeks swollen with cotton batting
the faces passing above like pages of old photographs
the old people in the back rows
the strangers who weep for strangers
the pallbearers moonlighting nephews through business school
the fat hungry face of the motorcycle cop
the siren's last stuttering vowels

THANKSGIVING

I was a boy stubborn with whisky as she walked
up a midway of lights & blew me a kiss off red nails
& the Confederate flag sewn to her G-string burned
in my eyes as I waited cold outside the stage door
in love with the promise.

The morning was Thanksgiving & I carved my name in oak
& ate in a grease café winking at the waitress & all morning
the beating of wings in my blood & the wind off the river
burned my face as I stood reading the city's glistening ciphers
to understand the mystery of the flesh & later
the day turned the gray of wash hanging in back yards
as I strutted the train aisle like a soldier returning
from the bliss of holy first contact & the Bible salesman
from Utah offered his best Gideon for the Confederate flag
pinned to my sleeve as I stood in the blast between cars waving
to an old woman rocking on a porch who I believed understood why
everywhere the light added my dimension to the studded air.

DARWIN, TORTOISES, GALAPAGOS ARCHIPELAGO & NEW HAMPSHIRE

For John & Mary

Darwin believed it his fate no sooner to discover
what was most interesting than to leave it; in other words:
to leave always before being left. He was young & full of odd ideas.
He smoked Turkish cigarettes on moonlit beaches watching natives balance
themselves on tortoises & noted the shells were shaped like the islands
of the Galapagos Archipelago. He wore tweed & carried Swiss binoculars.
He pursued the male tortoise through swamps & hot rains toward the female
who welcomed him by drawing in her head & tail & playing dead.
He listened to the godawful bellowing that edged her into the light
& noted that the stench carried over the islands like a sexual wind
that drew buzzards ecstatic for the white spherical eggs she buried
in the spongy surf. He believed in the instincts of passion
& the consequence of numbers. In the small act & the importance
of buzzards; in other words: posterity. I wonder if he ever got lonely
for phenomena he couldn't measure? What he dreamed in the long hours
before dawn when the human brain spins like a jellyfish
in the hard surf off Charles Island? If all that noting owned him
as he owned what he noted; in other words: fate. Once in a bar in Chicago
I swore off love. I was young & full of odd ideas.
I didn't know how black the nights get here in New Hampshire,
where the human heart drags through the mud of a hundred islands
like a tortoise inching toward something perhaps splendid.
I believe in the splendid. In the buzzards & eggs.
I believe most of all in the eggs & Dear Lord,
if I am what must last in this shell of a body give me the fate
written in the design of my face; in other words: the impossible balancing acts
here in the black nights of New Hampshire.

CÉZANNE

These old men stamp cold feet like turkeys
ruffling ragged feathers & talk of VA hospitals
& Japanese transistors as if talk were a grip on time.
One has cheekbones round as teacups & owl-stark eyes
that roll each time he coughs his upper teeth loose.
The other, wrapped in army surplus, smiles like a Pekinese
while tuning a radio pitted like a chicken coop. They've come
for the Cézanne show but I doubt the old master would wait hours
in a line that inches forward like a caterpillar fighting its own weight.
God knows what they expect. Color is the tree inside the tree & the skull
in the mountain of night but life in a veterans' hospital must be deadly
& soon winter will drop its dark lonely tonnage on our heads.
The truth is I've come begging. As a boy I climbed a chair to touch
the *Apples & Oranges* & in my room mixed colors to make the fire
that cut like knives. The old Frenchman with his oil-stained beard
& the spider's web of color shining in his eye—could he have guessed
that on a morning when the sky has grayed to the cold density of ash
& the world itself seems to have been stripped of its last string of color
so many men & women would line up five bodies deep to see the skies
& mountains & trees that are so red & blue & yellow we feel a splendor
that is the passion & the pain & the mystery of our lives?

LAUGHTER

One night my father yanked a tablecloth
from under my face & plates spun like meteors
as he wrapped it over his shoulders & his bald head lit up
like a pumpkin as he waltzed my mother round our crooked house
& tears soaked my collar & my stomach jumped into my mouth
as they flew chair over sofa & the world was a moment so full of us
I think of the Samurai playing with a daisy as he waits for his enemy
& only the daisy & the bright summer sun in his smile & I ask you
if at a time like this you would wonder if there was a beginning or end
with angels gathering on the roof to hear such loud tearing
at the fiery curtain of human delight.

MAIN STREETS

These are the days that must happen to you.
WALT WHITMAN

1

I wake from hours of water,
cats screaming for perfection,
the old woman upstairs lowered
into bed by God with a nasal cough
& one good leg. Already
the nearest bar loud with gorillas.

I wake, he wakes, we wake, they.
I would forget this city's name
if I could remember it. In three days
Christmas, the world full
of good will.

2

Who said longing knew night from day?
Success a tooth that can't be filled,
this morning the sun stabbed me in the back;
fate a horny cowboy undecided
which house to burn, which jaw to break.
Bad signs, Mama,

pour the soup, I'm on my way,
believe me, a new day,
why should he lie?

3

Twenty-two bars in town,
the same sad-toothed waitress works them all.
A man could go mad singing God Bless Our Home.
I'd leave this place if I could stand.

They hung Christmas three weeks before Thanksgiving.
Even the johns caw Rudolph down your throat
& the counters at Woolworth's go on forever
into summer at least.

4

My front window opens
on Saturday afternoon, drinkers waltz
down Burdick Street, one old father
this noon opened his fly
for an old mother lugging laundry,
she spat at it, Act you age, she said.

Always the next morning,
time to feed the cats who want in
so they can want out, this country
has no traditions, I think,
just connected Main Streets.

5

Maggie's Better Half, I can't recall
the dancehall's name, call it needing
somewhere to be, God what bone-smashing
electric twitching, one lady fainted,
you can't blame her, we're not
of this world by choice.

The Midwest one long winter,
Russian Jews not allowed on the Mall at night,
probably for good reason.

6

Friday night heroes lugging bellies up Main Street
with no wars, but wives to fight. Memorial Day
they sell flags at the cemetery & sleep it off
under lilacs imported from Japan.

Once it was all money & girls, their eyes say,
now the war is getting out of bed,
the mirror's cold dare, what is called
bare necessity: exact change & the daily dread
which, like drums, gets louder every year.

7

Picked up a little number
last night, she said, You
dangerous man you, only
seventeen her hands did
all the talking, my need
showed its teeth, Relax, she said,
you only live once, so
the next morning the last
taste sweet but fading,
like all dirty old men
I expect the police.

8

School children spit back my words by rote.
I sell words but words aren't bibles. Not everyone
wants them bound in gold leaf. Not everyone sings.

One year I drove an old Checker, no heater,
no dash lights, spent the winter
delivering old women from last calls,
one said, Driver, my dog just died, bango,
just like that, don't stop till you hit water.

A drunk swore he loved me, loved my cab,
but wouldn't get out. I stopped on railroad tracks,
left the motor running, never went back.

9

First light
moves down the new leaves
of my wandering Jew. I lie in bed
thinking dust dust & dust, adding up
what I owe myself in arrears.

Mornings like this
I wake hating
the Golden Gate Bridge.

10

Pigeons,
fat as gypsies, coo on the roof.
Vork vork vork cries my guardian angel, Stein.
But a little caterwaul fills the brain
with inspiring blood. Look,
my hands are ringing like castanets!

Why is everyone I know
such a moody
sonuvabitch?

11

The State Theater blinks
at Rex's Grill, which floats
on a liquored haze. A man
could cross this country
inside giant shopping malls
& never see daylight.

The spirit finds its own step.
I know Marilyn Monroe is dead,
that I'm not the first man on the moon,
the grinding in my groin tells me so. Mama,
I've been drinking again, storefronts sprint
& speakers hum Thanksgiving morning noon & night.

12

Nights
the red moon drops
close enough to polish
with spit.

THE GIFT

THE GIFT

For Ralph Dickey, 1945–1972

All that night the sere-faced moon drifted
through gray islands of sky as we tightroped
the reservoir's edge tossing stones & listening
for the tiny handclaps of water & later
we went down to the frozen river where he hopped one-legged
over cracking water with such laughter I think
he believed we would live forever in our bodies.

He never saw his black father
& his blond mother left him when his hair curled to wool
& he was left again when his almond-colored flesh turned cinnamon
& again until a black mother said with hands like his
he must play piano & nights he jammed with old black men
in tenement basements tapping his foot & keeping time with spoons
& it was so good, this music, it lifted him right out of his body.

There were nights he would call late & play something new
& hang up without hello or good-by & the air rang electric
& this morning I saw his face in every face in a crowd
& wished I could have told him the mystery of our lives unfolding,
the eyes of these women, their bodies coats of such blossoming color.

His body was found in the back seat of an old VW
parked on a cliff by the Pacific & a plastic bag
was wrapped round his head like the stocking he wore to flatten his hair
& his stomach was shredded with snail poison & his hands,
his hands large as Rachmaninoff's, were frozen to his throat
as if to feel the last singing breath.

51

CARL A. RUDISILL LIBRARY
LENOIR-RHYNE UNIVERSITY

One night I drove to those cliffs
where, below, the surf burns blue in the moonlight
& breaks yellow on black sand with the clap
of a thousand gulls being thrown up from the earth
& I sat hunched like a gutted crab in the burning salt spray
under a sky that hangs so low the lights of heaven
pressed on my head like a jeweled crown & all night
the human cry of gulls who suddenly break open their wings
& drop at fish heads flashing gold in foam & the black sun
splitting the dawn sky like an ax through hard wood
tossing splinters of flame across the horizon's fiery edge
& I rolled with the roll of the earth against water
everywhere returning the gift of light to light.

How, for a moment, a blink of time,
the whole world seemed lit from within
with a music that was fire, air, earth & water,
the gift of which, like the spines of grass he lies under,
sings & threads the wind.

CARL A. RUDISILL LIBRARY
LENOIR RHYNE

LIKE WINGS

For Marie

Last night I dreamed I was the first man to love a woman
& woke shaking & went outside to watch
the faded rag of the sky burn into dawn.
I am tired of the river before feeling,
the joy we must carve from shadow,
tired of my road-thick tongue.

I cannot hand you my breath or wrap the horizon
round your wrist & be forgiven.
I cannot rub the dry wood of my ribs to fire
& sleep. The edge of sleep isn't sleep.
I go room to room tying my feelings into knots.
The space we filled now fills me.
The light & dark won't mix.

I cannot leave myself like a house frozen in the background.
I am this body & the weather all year round.
I think of the light that opened over you our first morning,
how the glass in my lungs turned to sound
& I saw you woman & child & couldn't breathe, for love.
Fear is the edge that is the risk that is loving.
It stinks of blood, draws sharks.

The nights you waltzed naked round our bed,
myself holding the chair I'd painted blue again,
the cats flowing in the wings of your good yellow hair.
There is much men don't know about women,
how your hands work the air to water, the seed to life,
why the salt at the tips of your breasts glows
& tastes of mollusk.

There are hours when the future gives up all hope
& stops in the middle of busy streets
& doesn't care. But think of the distance we have come,
the hands which have wound us.
There will be others.

I have read of ancient people
who held razors to their doctor's throat
as he operated—as if love could have such balance,
like wings.

One night I followed your tracks through deep snow
& stood in an old schoolhouse watching the new sun
come red & shimmer over the opening fields,
the world white & flat & a light
I'd known all my life burned in my head like a fist of rags,
how I couldn't remember what we feared
we'd taken or left,
my arms opened to your shape, how I couldn't lift
out of my body, my mouth frozen
round the sound of your name.

FOR MY FATHER

Samuel Schultz, 1903–1963

Spring we went into the heat of lilacs
& his black eyes got big as onions & his fat lower lip
hung like a bumper & he'd rub his chin's hard fur on my cheek
& tell stories: he first saw America from his father's arms
& his father said here he could have anything if he wanted it
with all his life & he boiled soap in his back yard & sold it door to door
& invented clothespins shaped like fingers & cigarette lighters
that played *Stars & Stripes* when the lid snapped open.

Mornings he lugged candy into factories
& his vending machines turned peanuts into pennies
my mother counted on the kitchen table & nights he came home
tripping on his laces & fell asleep over dinner & one night
he carried me outside & said only God knew what God had up His sleeve
& a man only knew what he wanted & he wanted a big white house
with a porch so high he could see all the way back to Russia
& the black moon turned on the axis of his eye & his breath
filled the red summer air with the whisky of first light.

The morning his heart stopped I borrowed money to bury him
& his eyes still look at me out of mirrors & I hear him kicking
the coalburner to life & can taste the peanut salt on his hands
& his advice on lifting heavy boxes helps with the books I lug town to town
& I still count thunder's distance in heartbeats as he taught me & one day
I watched the sun's great rose open over the ocean as I swayed on the bow
of the Staten Island Ferry & I was his father's age when he arrived
with one borrowed suit & such appetite for invention & the bridges
were mountains & the buildings gold & the sky lifted backward
like a dancer & her red hair fanning the horizon & my eyes burning
in a thousand windows & the whole Atlantic breaking at my feet.

22057602 12|13 VISITING WRITER